Pinkalicious

Flower Girl

HARPER FESTIVAL
An Imprint of HarperCollinsPublishers

by Victoria Kann

For Libby!
xox,
Aunt Victoria

The author gratefully acknowledges
the artistic and editorial contributions
of Robert Masheris and Justine Fontes.

HarperFestival is an imprint of HarperCollins Publishers.

Pinkalicious: Flower Girl
Copyright © 2013 by Victoria Kann
PINKALICIOUS and all related logos and characters are trademarks of Victoria Kann
Used with permission.
Based on the HarperCollins book *Pinkalicious*
written by Victoria Kann and Elizabeth Kann, illustrated by Victoria Kann
All rights reserved. Printed in the United States of America.
No part of this book may be used or reproduced in any manner whatsoever without
written permission except in the case of brief quotations embodied in critical articles and reviews.
For information address HarperCollins Children's Books,
a division of HarperCollins Publishers, 195 Broadway, New York, NY 10007.
www.harpercollinschildrens.com

Library of Congress catalog card number: 2012942504
ISBN 978-0-06-218766-6

Book design by Kirsten Berger
15 16   CWM   10
❖
First Edition

Mommy was on the phone. I saw her smile and heard her say something about "a flower girl."

I wondered to myself, "What's a flower girl?"

My mind filled with pinkatastic visions of flower girls. It was positively pinkerrific! I wanted to be a flower girl! I was going to start making my outfit right away!

I rounded up some useful supplies. My green tights were good for my stem. Then all I had to make were the perfect petals!

Peter asked, "What are you doing?"
I told him, "I'm a flower girl!"
"Wow," Peter said. "Can I be a flower boy?
I want to be a tiger lily because it
sounds ferocious!"

"I'm a fragrant rose," I said, squirting Mommy's perfume all over me.

As soon as our outfits were done, Peter and I rushed out into the sunshine.

Peter ran around yelling "Look out—I'm a flower! I'm a tiger lily!"

I twirled around. "Look how delicate my petals are! Don't I smell rosealicious?" I said.

"What are you doing? And what is that smell?" asked Daddy.

I was surprised that he couldn't tell just by looking at us. "Haven't you ever seen flower children before? I am a flower girl and Peter is a flower boy."

Daddy chuckled. "Mommy will tell you later, but flower girls don't smell or look like flowers—they *throw* flowers."

I was shocked. "Are you sure?"

Daddy laughed. "Yes, it's true. Flower girls really throw flowers."

Peter and I were stunned. I asked, "Why would flower girls throw flowers?"

Peter shrugged, then started picking flowers and tossing them all over the lawn.

I was completely confused. "People throw balls and sometimes horseshoes, or even tantrums. Why would anyone throw flowers? That just doesn't make sense!" I said.

Then it came to me! "Maybe Daddy meant *flour*, not flowers!" I shouted as I hurried into the kitchen.

"I don't get it," said Peter.
I shrugged and said, "Neither do I."

Throwing flour didn't make any more sense than throwing flowers, but it sure was fun! There was flour everywhere! It looked like there had been a blizzard inside the kitchen.

Peter laughed. "It's like having a snowball fight, but without the cold fingers!"

When Mommy walked into the kitchen, we both froze.

She stared at us. She stared at the room. It was a mess! Mommy was speechless.

Finally she said, " Umm . . . what *are* you doing?"

When I told her, Mommy laughed so hard her face turned pink.
Then she explained what a flower girl is—and told me I was going
to be one very soon! "My cousin wants you to be the flower girl at her
wedding. Isn't that great?"

Being a flower girl was even better than I had imagined. I was part of the wedding party, and I LOVE parties! I got to wear a pinkatastic dress, and I got to throw petals when the bride walked down the aisle. Peter got to be a ring bearer, which has NOTHING to do with bears. It means he got to carry the wedding rings. But the very best part . . .

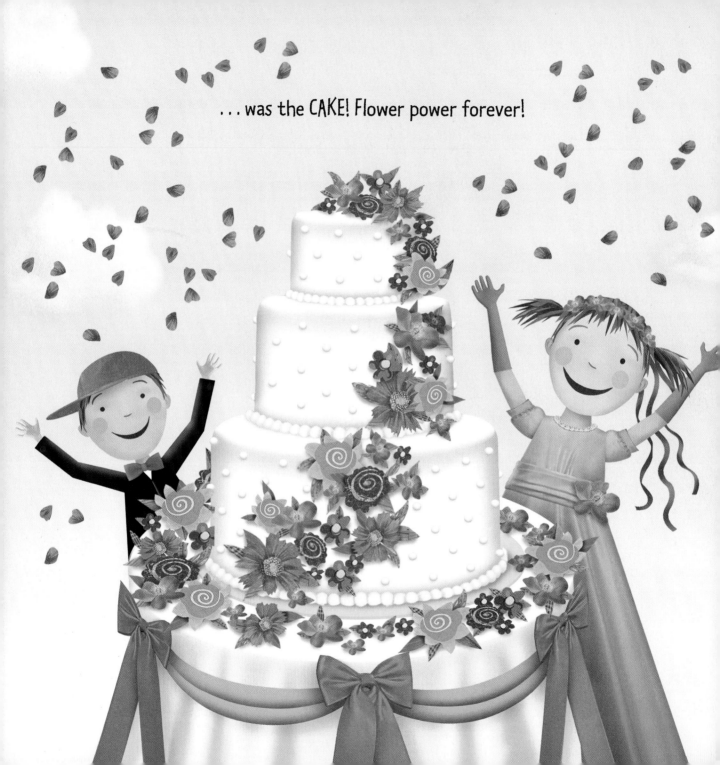

. . . was the CAKE! Flower power forever!